THE MAN
IN THE LITTLE YELLOW
Canoe

ADVENTURES WITH DUCHESS

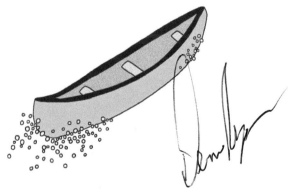

STORY BY DENNIS RYAN
ILLUSTRATIONS BY KENNADY OSBORNE

 FriesenPress

One Printers Way
Altona, MB R0G 0B0
Canada

www.friesenpress.com

ISBN
978-1-5255-5707-1 (Hardcover)
978-1-5255-5708-8 (Paperback)
978-1-5255-5709-5 (eBook)

1. JUVENILE FICTION, ANIMALS, DOGS

Distributed to the trade by The Ingram Book Company

For my children and grandchildren

It was early June when I first launched my canoe into the lake. I worked hard all year in shop classes building my canoe, and now was ready to enjoy the fruits of my labours.

As I glided through the water, my chest swelled with pride. The canoe ran straight and true when I paddled. With the sun beating down on my back, and the cool water beneath me, I just knew this summer was going to be perfect.

I had gotten a job as a ramp hand for a float-base operator that flew airplanes off the water in northern Ontario. Ramp hands did all the hard work, like fueling and washing the planes, along with weighing the cargo and passengers. We had to make sure the airplanes were safe for flying. It was a very important job.

Since I wanted to be close to work and the opportunity for adventure, I decided to live in a tent on McKenzie Island with my dog Duchess. The island was a short but sometimes rough canoe ride to the mainland.

Duchess was an old English sheepdog. I trained her to be obedient which helped a lot while we did our weekly adventures around the island. In the mornings, we woke up to the sounds of songbirds, and in the evenings, we had campfires under the starry night sky.

McKenzie Island was named after an old gold miner from the 1800s named Mr. McKenzie. He also ran the Hudson's Bay Company post on the island. He sold everything that was needed to survive the harsh northern Ontario winters.

There was also an abandoned gold mine on the island.

Mr. McKenzie and the local natives had a dispute over some goods at the Hudson's Bay post. The natives decided to run Mr. McKenzie off the island. It was said that, before this happened, Mr. McKenzie hid barrels of rum and cases of gold somewhere on the island. He did not want the natives to get his precious rum or gold.

On my days off, Duchess and I went looking for that rum and gold. While we were hunting for lost treasures, we found some good fishing areas. We could catch fish for supper whenever we wanted.

I worked weekends, with Mondays and Tuesdays off. My little yellow canoe took me to work every day. I felt bad leaving Duchess behind; she looked at me with her big brown eyes, which said, "Don't go!"

The mornings were my favourite time of the day. The waters were mostly calm, and it made for a smooth canoe ride. When the sun rose over the water, the sky and lake were transformed into hues of pink and orange.

Duchess was always sad to see me leave, but excited to see the little yellow canoe making its way back at the end of my long workday.

Every evening before dinner, I took Duchess for a walk and then for a short canoe ride. She was a big shaggy dog and she looked out of place sitting on her seat in the little yellow canoe.

Duchess was a bit nervous at first in the small boat, but she soon became very comfortable. She would sit on the seat just like I did. When the water got rough, she lowered her body off the seat and sat on the floor of the canoe. This was a great idea and I took up the same practice. Sitting on the bottom kept our weight low in the canoe and made it safer to paddle in rough weather. This also allowed us to go out onto the lake when the waves were high. My little canoe still felt stable in the rough waters.

I canoed every day to work and back. The local people knew me as the man in the little yellow canoe.

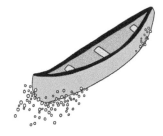

One day at work, I found an old map of McKenzie Island tucked away inside an old book. The map showed all the bays, rivers, and creeks that ran through the island. I asked the boss if I could borrow it for the summer, and he said okay. Now I had a map that I could use to plan a thorough search for where Mr. McKenzie may have hidden his treasure.

I studied the map and found the location of the old abandoned gold mine not far from our campsite.

The next morning was my day off, so I gathered some supplies and loaded up the yellow canoe. Duchess jumped into the bow, and we started off on our first big adventure in search of lost gold.

We paddled along the shoreline, scanning for any signs of a path to the old gold mine.

It was cool at first, but our faces started to warm up when the sun rose in the sky. The bottom of the lake was mostly sandy, but in one spot, I noticed there were a lot of pebbles. The bush line opened up to a small trail. Was the gold mine close?

I steered the canoe onto the shore and tied it off. Duchess bounded out of the canoe, barking excitedly, beckoning me to follow. There were signs of an old trail that ended at the water's edge. This looked like a good place to start our search.

We followed the winding trail, placing red ribbons on the trees along the way so that we could find our way back to the canoe.

After walking inland for a half hour, we came upon the entrance to the old gold mine.

Duchess got very excited when she saw the mine entrance. She ran right in, and I followed.

It quickly got dark, and I didn't have a flashlight. The mine shaft started off with a gentle decline, but soon became a slippery slope that went down to nowhere. Duchess was way ahead of me, barking and panting. I don't know how she could see, but I knew we couldn't go much farther. I called Duchess to come and soon she was back at my side. We felt our way back to the entrance of the cold, damp tunnel. We would need to explore this mine another day, and I would have to remember to bring a flashlight next time. I also figured that Mr. McKenzie probably didn't hide his gold in a gold mine.

Duchess ran off again as soon as we got out of the mine. I could hear her barking excitedly a little ways off, so I ran to see what she had discovered. I found her outside an old mining shack. The door lock was rusted, so it didn't take much force to open it. We found ourselves in the main room. In the corner, there was an open safe. Inside, there were several cylindrical rocks, each about the size of a cucumber. They were old mine samples.

I loaded up my back pack with a few samples, so that I could get them checked out. There were different colours of very hard stone. ***Could there be gold in the samples?*** What did gold look like in the natural stone? I only knew that it was shiny and somewhat soft to the touch. I had a gold chain given to me by my mom, and these samples did not look like that.

We walked back to the canoe along the same trail. I took down all the red ribbons I had placed on the trees. We did not want to make it easy for anybody else to find this mine. Duchess and I knew exactly where it was, and we could use the ribbons on our next adventure.

After collecting the samples, my stomach started to grumble. We'd had a busy morning, so before heading back home, I decided to unpack the food I had brought. Duchess and I sat down for a ham sandwich and a special homemade doughnut. These doughnuts were made by a lady on the mainland who knew that Duchess loved them as much as I did. She knew about our weekly adventures, and made sure we had fresh doughnuts every Monday morning.

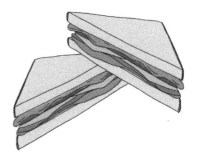

After lunch, we got in the canoe and paddled back to the tent. We hadn't found McKenzie's gold, but didn't care. We had a fun day of exploring, and knew that we had the entire summer ahead of us to search the island. I knew, as I stretched out beneath the starry sky, that today was the first adventure of many for Duchess and me and our little yellow canoe.

A word from the owner of the
little yellow canoe

Many years ago, I told stories to my kids about my experiences working as a ramp hand in northern Ontario. I told them about my little yellow canoe, my dog Duchess, my cat, and all the people we met.

Later, I learned how to fly, and my children got to hear more of my adventures. My kids turned into parents, and the stories started all over again with my grandchildren. This time, I wrote down my adventures in little handwritten books bound together with duct tape. This allowed my grandchildren to read the stories back to me. They asked all kinds of questions, especially about Duchess. How big was she? What did she look like? I found an artist, and we put the words and pictures together. Before I knew it, I had written and published my first children's book.

These stories recount my adventures paddling around in my little yellow canoe in northern Ontario. As these events took place over forty years ago, my memory may have affected some of the storylines slightly. This is the first of many adventures, and I'm not yet ready to reveal the answer to my grandson Lukas's biggest question: Did Duchess and I ever find the gold?

Stay tuned for more adventures!

About the Author

A long time ago, author and pilot Dennis Ryan was the man in the little yellow canoe, working as a ramp hand up North, where he lived in a tent with his English sheepdog. His memories of that time in his life became the inspiration for the stories he told his children—stories that were then told by his children to his grandchildren.

Dennis currently lives in Sarnia, Ontario with his wife, Judy, and Sparky the cat.

About the Artist

Kennady Osborne has been inspired by the arts and creative process since a very young age. She developed her artistic skills at the Ontario College of Arts and Design. She finds inspiration as she delves deep into the story-telling cultures of her rich Mohawk and Scottish ancestors. Kennady loves to encourage others to find their voice through self-expression and promote creativity by sharing stories and knowledge. She now owns and operates Seventh Rayn Design in her hometown of Corunna, Ontario where she lives with her two dogs.

NORTHERN BIRDS INDEX

COMMON RAVEN

NORTHERN GOSHAWK

GREY JAY

FOX SPARROW

GREAT GREY OWL

WHITE WINGED CROSSBILL

PALM WARBLER

RED BREASTED NUTHATCH

BUFFLE HEAD

RUSTY BLACKBIRD

HAWK OWL

BOREAL CHICKADEE

SPRUCE GROUSE

EVENING GROSBEAK

SANDHILL CRANE

PILEATED WOODPECKER

HERMIT THRUSH

Did you find these birds hidden in the story?

Each page has one of these northern birds.

9 781525 557088